This book belongs to:

First published 2005 by Walker Books Ltd
87 Vauxhall Walk, London SE11 5HJ

This edition published 2007

2 4 6 8 10 9 7 5 3 1

Illustrated in the style of Lucy Cousins by King Rollo Films Ltd

"Maisy" audio visual series produced by King Rollo Films Ltd
for Universal Pictures International Visual Programming

Printed in China

British Library Cataloguing in Publication Data:
a catalogue record for this book is
available from the British Library

ISBN 978-1-4063-0047-5
www.walkerbooks.co.uk

Sweet Dreams, Maisy

Lucy Cousins

WALKER BOOKS
AND SUBSIDIARIES
LONDON • BOSTON • SYDNEY • AUCKLAND

The sun is shining bright.
It's a beautiful day!

Maisy plays outside
with Charley, Eddie,
Cyril and Tallulah.

At sunset,
the day ends.
It's time to
say goodbye.

Look at all the
colours in the sky.

The moon rises.
The stars begin to shine.
The world is going
to sleep.

The house is snug.
The house is warm.

Maisy reads a
story to Panda.

"Once upon a time ..."

Up, up, up
the stairs
climb Maisy
and Panda.

It's time
to go
to bed.

In bed Maisy sings to Panda.
"Twinkle, twinkle,
little star."

Moonlight,
moonshine,
it's a beautiful
night!

Go back to
bed, Maisy.
Sleep tight,
sweet dreams...

Silver moon and twinkling stars, shine your light on Maisy.